THE BALLERINA

STRETCHING THE LIMITS

SHAE'S T-GIRL ADVENTURES
BOOK 5

VICTORIA RUSH

VOLUME 5

SHAE'S T-GIRL ADVENTURES - BOOK 5

COPYRIGHT

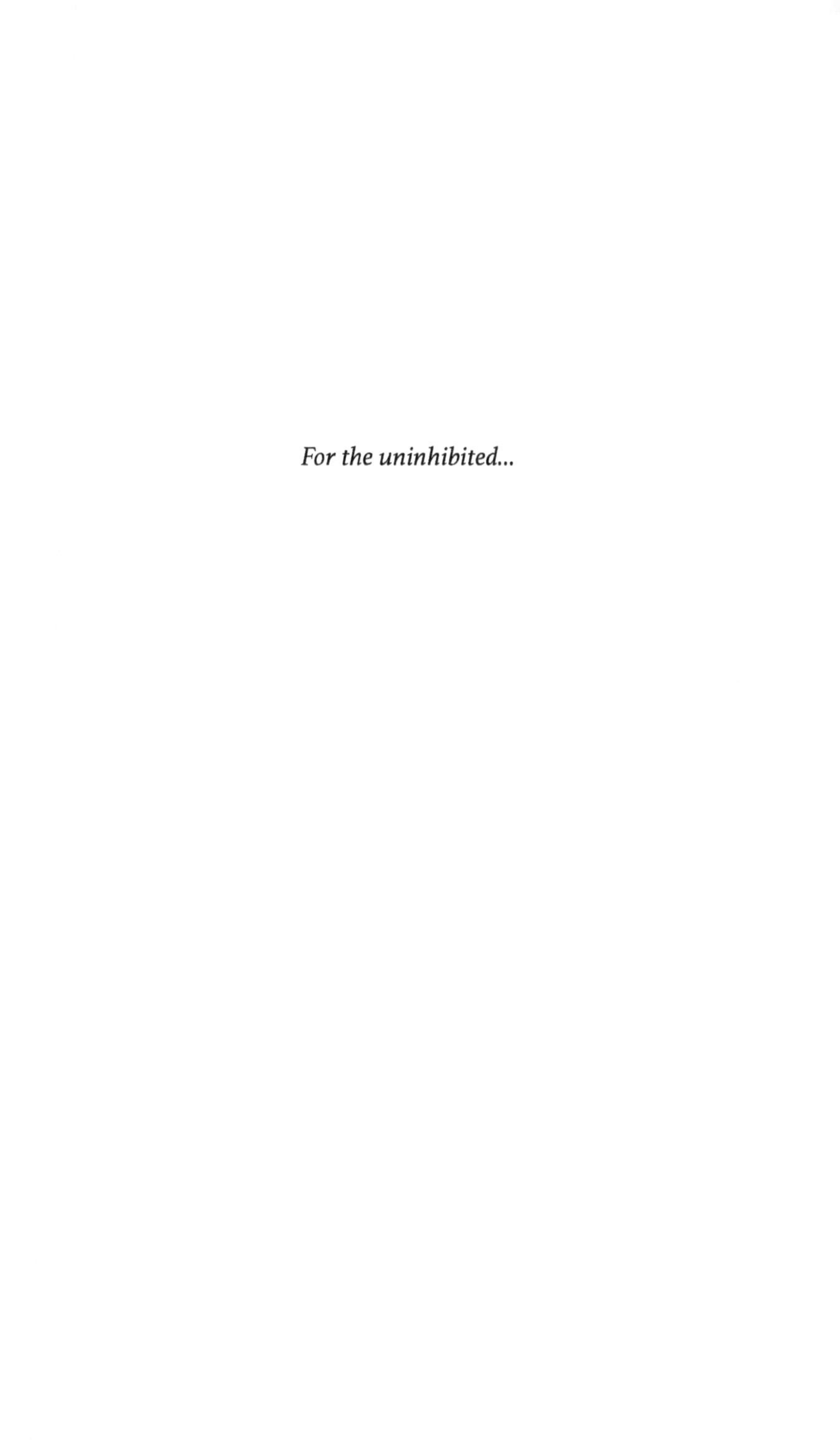

For the uninhibited...

1

———

I'd been looking forward to this performance of Swan Lake for weeks. My friend Jade had invited me to the new production of the Joffrey Ballet at the Lyric Opera House for my thirtieth birthday, and as the evening of the presentation rapidly approached, I was in a tizzy for what I should wear. As I flipped through the rows of clothes hanging in my walk-in closet, I blew the hair off my sweaty forehead with a huff of my lower lip, becoming increasingly frustrated. I hadn't dressed up in ages, and the few gowns that I owned seemed too dressy for a sit-down affair. Just as I pulled a black pantsuit off one of the hangers, my cell phone rang atop my bed in the next room and I saw Jade's name pop up on the screen.

"Hey," I answered with a telltale sigh.

"Did I catch you at a bad time?" Jade said, recognizing my distress.

"I'm getting a bit nervous about tonight's date," I said. "I can't figure out what to wear. I haven't been to a fancy shindig like this in a while. Is a pantsuit too low-key for this kind of gathering?"

"That could work," Jade said. "But this is a premiere performance for the ballet company. Most people dress up for this sort of thing."

"Even though we're going to be sitting in the *dark* for most of the evening?"

"We won't be hiding in the dark for the entire evening. Everybody will be paying close attention to the guests' entrances. This is as close as our city gets to the Met Gala. It's a chance to show off your best style while flaunting your arm candy. Plus, there will be a fair amount of mingling in the cocktail lounge during the intermission, and you never know who you might bump into. There are quite a few high-profile dignitaries who show up to these first-run performances."

"Speaking of arm candy," I said, crossing my arms. "Everybody will be looking at you, anyway. You fill out a dress way better than me."

"It depends which part of the dress people are looking at," Jade teased. "You've got some extra curves in places I can only dream about."

"Yeah, well, I try to keep those under wraps until they're absolutely needed. I'm not sure all those haughty big-wigs will appreciate a *tranny* showing up for their big coming-out party."

"Maybe you can give them a little taste of what they're missing," Jade laughed. "Why don't you wear that silk ball gown with the slit up one side? Your legs are your best feature anyhow. Everybody will be so busy looking *down* that they'll hardly even notice the plunging necklines and fancy jewelry of all the other divas attending."

"That might work," I nodded, carrying my phone into my dressing room and pulling back the hangers framing my gown. "I'll have to pair it with the right accessories to make it stand out though. Black can be a little boring without the right shoes and handbag."

"I'm sure you can figure it out," Jade said. "Pick you up at eight?"

"Sounds good," I smiled. "Thanks again for the treat."

"Nothing but the best for my best girl," Jade said.

"And *boy*?" I grinned.

"When the mood suits," Jade chuckled.

"I better wear my compression panties then," I smiled. "With that big split up my side, there's no accounting for where my dick might wander while I'm sitting next to you."

"You better keep it under wraps, at least until after the show. Because where we'll be sitting, you'll be the center of attention."

At promptly eight p.m., Jade buzzed me from the lobby of my condominium building, and when I met her downstairs, her eyes flared open when she caught sight of my ensemble. I'd chosen black patent Christian Louboutin heels to go with my high-cut dress, along with a beaded red clutch purse and a ruby pendant necklace that nestled just above the top of my plunging neckline. To accentuate my cleavage in the tight-fitting dress, I wore a faux-sable black fur shawl pulled back off my shoulders.

"Wow," Jade said when she saw my outfit. "You look absolutely smashing this evening. I bet you'll be turning more than a few heads tonight."

"You're not too shabby yourself," I smiled, slipping my elbow under her arm as she escorted me outside toward our waiting cab. "That red sequin dress matches perfectly with my accent colors."

"I had a feeling you'd go with red," Jade nodded as she held the taxi door open for me while I climbed in the back. "We make the perfect couple, even when we're not joined together by certain other shiny red parts."

When we arrived at the opera hall, large spotlights circled the sky as freshly washed limousines stopped in front of the entrance steps while paparazzi flash bulbs flickered like fireworks around the distinguished arrivals. Our taxi pulled up behind a long limousine, and as we followed the entourage up the red-carpet-lined steps, we could hear the murmurs of the surrounding crowd as they commented on the famous faces they recognized.

"I'm glad I choose not to wear *skinny jeans* tonight," I chuckled to Jade as she gripped my arm tightly while I tried not to tip over on my six-inch-heels.

"You'd look good wearing a *potato sack* with a slit that high," she said, rubbing the side of her hip softly against mine. "I'm not sure if the spectators are more distracted by the sight of Taylor Swift or two sexy girls showing more skin than the latest episode of Orange is the New Black."

"I'm pretty sure it's Taylor Swift," I said, watching the singer's tight ass wiggling in her gold-lamé dress as she climbed up the steps ahead of us. "I'd fuck that ass any day of the week."

"You and me both, girl," Jade said as she squeezed my arm with her sweaty hand.

When we entered the portico of the opera house, one of the attendants clipped our tickets as he waved us into the foyer leading into the main auditorium. I noticed my ex-lover Aiden Brando standing in a group next to Taylor Swift, and when I caught his eye, he glanced at the slit in my dress, then at Jade, smiling knowingly.

"Friend of yours?" Jade said, noticing our brief exchange.

"Not anymore," I said, noticing a brunette wearing too much mascara standing next to him. "Looks like he's got a new distraction."

"Don't worry about those hotshots," Jade said, gripping my arm with two hands and leading me through the wide doors leading into the concert hall. "We've got everything we need right here to enjoy your special day."

I glanced up and turned my head as I admired the colonnaded walls and painted art nouveau ceiling of the giant opera hall while my heart pounded in my chest.

"Where are we sitting in this huge auditorium? It looks big enough to host a *hockey game.*"

"You'll see," Jade smiled as she escorted me further down the main aisle.

When we reached the front row next to the orchestra, I peered up at her with wide eyes while the attendant checked our tickets.

"The *front row*?" I said, flaring my eyes. "How did you manage to score seats so close to the stage? They must have cost you a small fortune!"

"Your thirtieth birthday only comes around once in a lifetime," she smiled, leading me to the two seats in the middle of the row, facing the front of the stage. "Besides, I know somebody on the inside who got me a special deal."

"Like the president or the artistic director?" I said, trying not to pay attention as Aiden and his group took their seats on the other side of our row.

"Something like that," Jade nodded as we took our seats and clasped our hands together excitedly.

As I listened to the buzz of the crowd flitting into the theater, I crossed my leg softly over my knee, revealing the side of my thigh directly in Aiden's line of sight. While he tried to ignore me, making small talk to his girlfriend and

Taylor Swift flanking him on his other side, I smiled while I felt my cock twitching under my tight underwear for the first time that evening.

This should be interesting, I thought to myself as I listened to the rumbling of props behind the curtain while the stage hands prepared the set for the first act of the performance. *It won't just be men in tights who'll be sporting bulges in their crotch tonight...*

2

———————

When the lights dimmed in the theater, a sudden hush fell over the audience, and the orchestra began playing the opening bars to Tchaikovsky's score. The curtains parted, displaying a park setting with a large palace in the background. A group of male dancers gathered together in a festive mood, with the lead actor dressed in a more ornate uniform dancing merrily among them to celebrate his birthday. An older gentleman in a dark robe entered from the side, appearing to offer the prince some guidance, and I peered at Jade with angled eyebrows.

"It's beautiful," I said. "But how can you follow the story?"

"That's what ballet is all about," she whispered. "It's interpretive dance. You're supposed to understand the interplay between the characters from their body language."

"Well, they certainly have beautiful bodies," I nodded, staring at the muscular thighs and bulging crotches of the male dancers as they glided gracefully across the stage. "Especially the one in the middle. I'm picking up some special vibes of my *own* from his body language."

"He's playing the role of Odette's love interest, Prince Siegfried. He's pretty hot, isn't he?"

"Yeah, but who's the guy in the dark robe?"

"He's the prince's tutor," Jade said, thrusting the playbill into my hand. "Why don't you read the story synopsis to follow the scenes for each act?"

I opened the pamphlet and read the brief outline for Act I, then I nodded, glancing back up at the stage. An older woman appeared on the stage, who began conversing quietly with the prince, then she introduced a series of pretty female dancers who performed for the prince's amusement, after which he weaved happily among them, giving none of them any extra attention.

"He doesn't seem particularly impressed by their dancing," I said, leaning toward Jade and elbowing her gently in her side.

"The queen is pressuring him to marry, but he hasn't found anyone deserving of his love," she whispered back.

"I'd offer *my* services if he was willing," I chuckled as I stared at the prince's ass. "Look at that magnificent backside. Have you ever seen such a perfectly carved butt?"

"It's pretty fine," Jade nodded. "No wonder all the other women are fawning over him."

"Is he growing aroused by their company?" I said, ogling his protruding package. "Or is he just naturally hung like that?"

"He's probably wearing a codpiece under his tights, but you never know," Jade grinned. "Maybe that's why he's the principal dancer."

While I watched the prince jumping and flexing his legs as he flitted between the scantily clad women, I could feel my panties slowly tightening in my crotch as my organ began to expand between my moistening labia. By the time

Act 1 finished with a flourish of paired performances between each of the participants, I could feel my panties becoming wet and I fanned my face with my hand as I peered at Jade.

"Whew," I said, flaring my eyes open in excitement. "Is it getting hot in here, or is it just me?"

"It's definitely warming up," Jade nodded as a loud buzz returned to the auditorium. "But we've got a front-row seat to all the action, so maybe we're feeling it a bit more than the others."

"Well, I'm *feeling* it alright," I said, squeezing my thighs together while trying to keep my swelling dick under control. "I don't suppose you brought any mini-pads with you tonight? I think I need to put something under my panties to keep me from creating a giant wet spot in the middle of my dress."

"By *wet spot*, I'm assuming you mean–"

"Boy juice, not girl stuff," I smiled. "That hot lead dancer is making more than just my legs tremble."

"You've got fifteen minutes before the start of the next act," Jade chuckled, handing me a pack of pads discreetly while I stuffed them into my purse. "You better make this quick before you miss the introduction of the other lead."

"No worries," I said, rising up from my seat and heading up the aisle past Aiden Brando as he glanced at the flaring slit in my dress.

Those dancers aren't the only ones with surprises under their tights, I smiled to myself as I felt my dick pulsing in excitement.

The ladies' room was more spacious than I imagined, and after finding an open stall, I cleaned up my premature emissions and inserted a mini-pad tightly between my folded penis and the front of my panties. Fortunately, my compression underwear had kept my ladyboy cock nicely concealed between the folds of my outer labia, and when I returned to my seat, I winked at Aiden when he glanced at the front of my dress as I walked past his entourage. By the time I returned to my seat, the lights were already starting to dim, and Jade looked at me with a raised eyebrow.

"Everything okay down there?" she said, peering into my lap.

"It is now," I smiled. "Your pad will help keep things better contained from now on."

"Let's hope so," she said. "The last thing we need is for you to start tenting the front of your dress to distract the performers on the stage."

"What's good for the goose is good for the gander," I said, making a not-too-subtle reference to the oversize crotches of the male ballet performers.

"Speaking of *birds*," she whispered, tilting her head in the direction of the stage as the curtains parted for the beginning of Act 2. "It looks like we've got a few new players coming onto the scene..."

I glanced up and noticed the set had changed to a nighttime scene at the side of a lake, where the prince was dancing furtively beside the shoreline with a bow in his hand while a group of swans glided quietly across the water. As he pointed his bow at the last one, who was about to disappear from view, suddenly a female dancer dressed in a white tutu emerged from the wings, and the prince paused, taken aback by her apparent transformation. As the ballerina danced across the stage in his direction while flapping her arms in the manner of a swan, I gasped at her beauty and graceful form.

"Is that *Odette*?" I said, leaning over toward Jade.

"Mm-hmm," she nodded, reaching out to grasp my trembling hand.

"She's stunning," I said, suddenly feeling my dick twitching for an entirely different reason. "It's like she's floating over the stage."

"That's why she's the female lead," Jade nodded. "Only the best get to perform in the lead role."

"Look at those *legs*," I hummed softly. "They seem to go on forever. And her *face*. She looks positively luminous..."

"That's Olga Antonova. She's on loan from the Kirov ballet. She's been captivating audiences in Russia for years."

"I can see why," I nodded, leaning forward unconsciously as she moved toward the front of the stage.

As I watched her fluttering across the platform while she lifted her arms and legs effortlessly into the air, I could feel my heart pounding in my chest the same way the male lead must have felt when he first laid eyes on the captivating beauty. When they finally joined their bodies together, their chemistry was unmistakable while they skirted around one another, then embraced tightly as the handsome prince raised her in the air and twirled her around in his arms.

"My God," I gushed to Jade, feeling my legs trembling while I watched the duo dancing tenderly. "Who needs a *program* when you have dancing like that?"

"Exactly," Jade nodded.

"I'd fall in love with her *too*, if she emerged from the lake in that form."

"It's not as simple as it seems," she said, nodding toward

the stage as the music took an ominous turn and a third character emerged from the wings, dressed in an owl costume. He danced around the periphery of the fledgling lovers, then he plunged between them, threatening the prince for Odette's attention.

"Who's *that*?" I said to Jade, wrinkling my forehead in surprise.

"The owl-sorcerer, Rothbart. He's the one who cast a spell on the swans, making them appear as birds during the day and women only at night."

I picked up the playbill again and quickly scanned the synopsis for Act 2, then I threw it down in my lap angrily.

"Well, that's not fair!" I huffed, furrowing my brow as I glared at the feather-figured dancer. "Who is he to get in the way of true love?"

"You seem to be losing yourself in the play," Jade chuckled softly. "Stay tuned, because it only gets more complicated from here."

I watched the pretty girl representing Odette whisper something into the prince's ear, then he turned to confront the evil sorcerer, with his movements showing he intended to harm his nemesis. But when Odette interceded and pleaded with the prince not to kill Rothbart lest his spell be made permanent, the sorcerer retreated into the shadows while the rest of Odette's friends emerged from the lake and joined her on the stage. For the next half hour, the band of white-skirted ballerinas put on a collective performance that took my breath away. While they tapped their feet and waved their arms together like a herd of perfectly choreo-graphed swans, the prince and Odette danced with increasing passion, building to the exciting climax where they fell into each other's arms, proclaiming their undying love for one another.

When the curtain went down to signal the first intermission, I stared at the stage like a child who'd just seen Santa Claus on Christmas Eve.

"Are you *alright* there, girl?" Jade said, squeezing my sweaty palm over the armrest separating our seats.

"I think so," I nodded while catching my breath. "That's the most beautiful production I've ever seen."

"Even without *subtitles*?" Jade chuckled.

"Who needs *words* when the dancers' movement expresses everything you need to know," I said.

"I'm glad you're embracing the art form," Jade said. "I wasn't sure when I invited you to the show if you'd enjoy ballet as much as some of the more traditional forms of entertainment."

"Are you *kidding* me?" I said. "With figures like that, music that transports you, and dancing that takes your breath away, this is way better than any movie or play I've ever seen."

"Maybe you could use a little break to catch your breath," Jade said, noticing my chest still heaving in excitement. "Why don't we make our way to the cocktail lounge for a drink and a little R&R? The third act won't start for another half hour."

"A martini on ice is just what I need right now," I said, watching Aiden Brando rise up from his seat at the opposite end of our row and hold out his hand to help his date out of her seat. "I'm feeling a bit of drama of my *own* that might require a certain dance to cut the tension–"

"Oh?" Jade said, glancing in Aiden's direction. "Is something dark coming between you and your true love?"

"I wouldn't exactly call it *true love*," I grinned. "Just someone who might need a reminder of what his current situation is lacking..."

3

J ade and I followed the crowd as they filtered out of their seats and made their way up the aisle toward the large lounge on the second floor of the opera house. When we arrived, there was a long lineup at the bar to order drinks, and I noticed Aiden and his new girlfriend chatting with one of the attendants. When we finally reached the counter, trying to get the attention of the bartender, Aiden noticed our frustration and he brought his date over to say hello.

"Shae," he said with his trademark smoldering smile. "It's so nice to see you again. Are you enjoying the show?"

"Very much," I nodded, trying not to stare at his girlfriend's Botox lips and obvious fake tits. "I didn't realize it was possible to be moved so much by a silent performance."

"Well, these performers have a special way of projecting their thoughts..."

"Indeed," I said, darting my eyes toward the giant diamond pendant hanging from his girlfriend's neck. "And their feelings."

"Excuse me," Aiden said, noticing his date shuffling impatiently next to him. "This is my partner, Gianna."

"Pleased to meet you," I smiled, holding out my hand to his date. "And this is my partner, Jade."

"Oh?" Aiden said, shaking Jade's hand politely. "Are you two an item?"

I glanced at Jade with a wicked smile and winked.

"We've never been called *that* before, have we?" I chuckled.

"I suppose there are a few times when you could say we're a single item," Jade grinned.

"How about you two?" I said, appraising his date more closely. Although she was fairly pretty, her shoulders were broader than most women's, and I noticed a small lump in her throat where a man's Adam's apple normally rested. "How long have you two been an *item*?"

"We've been seeing each other on and off for a while, but this is our first public outing," Aiden said, smiling at his date awkwardly.

"You seem to be making quite a splash,' I said, noticing other people milling about the bar peering at the couple out of the sides of their eyes while they whispered into each other's ears. I wasn't sure if it was because they recognized the handsome billionaire, or they were distracted by his date's gown that left little to the imagination. "Perhaps you should *come out* more often."

"I think we will," Aiden smiled, darting his eyes down toward the slit in my dress while I noticed a slight bulge in his trousers. "Can I get you girls something to drink? I might be able to get to the front of the line if you're in a hurry to get back to your seats."

"That would be lovely," I nodded. "I'll have a Grey Goose martini, straight up."

"I prefer a *wet pussy*, thank you," Jade said without a hint of irony.

"Um, okay..." Aiden said, flaring his eyes in surprise. He raised his hand and snapped his finger, and one of the bartenders quickly moved to our end of the counter.

"What can I get you, Mr. Brando?" the bartender said.

"One Grey Goose martini and one wet pussy," Aiden said, lowering his voice so the other bystanders couldn't hear him. "And another strawberry daiquiri for the lady."

"Coming right up," the bartender nodded, returning to the other side of the bar to mix the drinks.

When he returned and handed us our drinks, Aiden motioned to the large group milling in the corner of the lounge, next to Taylor Swift and her boyfriend.

"Would you like to meet my friend, Taylor Swift?" he said.

I peered over in the direction of the group, watching couples jostling for position while trying to get selfies with the famous singer.

"Maybe another time," I said, hearing the soft chime of scale tones coming from the orchestra, signaling it was time to return to our seats for the beginning of the next act. "It looks like she's getting plenty enough attention during this brief intermission."

"No worries," Aiden nodded, placing his hand under Gianna's lower back and guiding her back in the direction of their group. "It was nice meeting you both this evening. Maybe we'll see you again another time."

"Perhaps at the next performance," I said, smiling at his date as her gemstone glistened inches above her inflated tits.

~

When Jade and I finished our drinks, we returned to the front row at the same time Aiden and his entourage took their seats on the other end of the aisle. I noticed his date sitting down carefully so as not to rumple the front of her dress, then she crossed her legs slowly while shifting her hips uncomfortably in her chair.

"You were very naughty back there," Jade smiled when she sat down next to me, noticing me glancing in their direction.

"What about *you*?" I said, elbowing her in the side. "Ordering a wet pussy of all things."

"It was a not-so-subtle diss at your boyfriend's date. Was it as obvious to you as it was to me that she was a little more than she pretended?"

"The Adam's apple always gives it away," I nodded. "I guess he has a thing for ladyboys."

"Except I think that one's had a little more work to make her look like a *lady* instead of a boy."

"Maybe," I chuckled. "But the top half seems to make up for whatever shortcomings she may have on the bottom."

"Yeah, those fake breasts were virtually *spilling* out of her gown."

"The rest of the crowd didn't seem to mind," I laughed. "Just as many people were staring at her big bosom as they were at Taylor Swift's groupies."

Suddenly, the lights in the theater dimmed, and the orchestra struck up the opening number to the next scene. When the curtains parted, the set displayed a grand ballroom, where Prince Siegfried appeared next to his mother, who presented a series of dancing maidens as candidates for his upcoming marriage. The sorcerer Rothbart arrived in disguise with his daughter, Odile, who was transformed to look like Odette. The prince was smitten once again, and although the maidens tried to attract him with their dances, he only had eyes for Odile. While the duo danced an exuberant pas de deux, displaying their passion for one another, Odette suddenly appeared at the castle window attempting to warn the prince of Rothbart's subterfuge, but he doesn't see her. Siegfried then proclaims to the court that he will marry Odile before Rothbart shows him the magical vision of Odette. Grief-stricken and realizing his mistake, the prince rushes back to the lake.

The more I watched the performance, the more pulled into the story I became, feeling my heart pounding whenever the Prince and Odette appeared together and the hairs raising on my arms whenever the evil sorcerer appeared. By the time the third act finished, I felt a thin film of sweat forming on my forehead while I clenched the armrests of my seat tightly with both hands.

"Hey," Jade said, sliding her hand softly over my white knuckles. "You know this is all make-believe. I wouldn't want you having a heart attack before the big finale."

"Well, they're certainly making *me* believe," I said. "I haven't seen such a compelling love story in a long time. All I can say is there better be a happy ending."

"It depends how you define a happy ending," Jade grinned, curling her fingers around mine as she squeezed them gently. "We've had quite a few of those ourselves in a different setting–"

"Yes," I said, feeling the blood suddenly rushing to a new part of my anatomy while I reflected back on our many trysts together. "You might have to give me some of your special loving when we're finished here tonight. I'm beginning to feel moved somewhere *else*..."

"Never fear," Jade smiled, sliding her fingers softly up the inside of my arm toward my darted nipples. "I've got a special surprise planned for you after the show. I promise not to disappoint you."

"Mmm," I hummed while rubbing my knee gently against hers. "I can't wait."

The curtains parted again, and the stage setting returned to the side of the lake. Odette appeared distraught while the swan maidens tried to comfort her. Siegfried returned and made a passionate apology, but it was too late, since his betrayal could not be reversed. As the couple performed one final bittersweet dance together, I felt the tears streaming down the front of my face, realizing their love could never be consummated.

Realizing she will remain a swan forever, Odette shows she wants to die. The prince chooses to die with her and they leap into the lake together. This breaks Rothbart's spell over the swan maidens, causing him to lose his power over them and he dies. In the final scene, the other swans are transformed back into regular maidens, and they watch as Siegfried and Odette ascend into the Heavens, forever united in love. When the curtains closed, I found myself heaving in despair as I clutched my hands together over my chest, rocking slowly back and forth in my chair.

"It wasn't such a bad ending," Jade said, wrapping her arms around my shoulders while trying to comfort me. "They were together in the end, and she was transformed into a real woman."

"But they weren't able to enjoy the rest of their life together on *Earth*!" I sobbed, staring at her with puffy eyes. "It ended just as it started—as a dreamy fantasy."

"Then the performers accomplished their goal," Jade smiled. "They moved you and made you feel their connection. You can't ask for anything else from a professional production."

"I need to see *more* of her," I sniffed. "That was the most beautiful thing I've ever witnessed. When is the principal dancer's next performance coming up?"

"You can see a little more of her right now if you want," Jade said, nodding toward the front of the stage as the curtains parted once again and the ballet performers rushed onto the stage in ascending order of importance while the audience cheered loudly.

When the duo representing Siegfried and Odette skipped onto the stage and joined hands, bowing together, I stood up, clapping wildly while my tears streamed all the way down to the cleft in my bosom.

"She's even more beautiful when she's *out of character*," I gushed, feeling my heart pounding in my chest as the dance glanced briefly in our direction. "I'd die and go to heaven *myself* if I had a chance to meet her in person."

"Well, I *did* say I had a little surprise for you at the end of the show, and it *is* your birthday–" Jade grinned while clasping my hand and nodding toward the lead dancer.

"What?" I said, noticing their brief interchange. "Do you *know* her?"

"We went to school together for a while," Jade nodded. "We've stayed in touch and remained friends. She's the one who arranged these special seats for us tonight."

"Really?" I said, widening my eyes. "I don't suppose–?"

"She agreed to meet us backstage after everything quiets down," Jade smiled. "Give her ten minutes or so to finish receiving the audience's attention, then we can join her in her dressing room."

"No way!" I gasped, jumping up and down in Jade's arms. "This is the best birthday present ever!"

"Even better than having a private audience with that *other* famous diva?" Jade said, tilting her head toward Taylor Swift and her group as they rose from their seats and began slowly heading out of the theater.

"Pfft!" I snorted, watching Aiden and his date following close behind the rest of the entourage, trying to soak up as much paparazzi attention as they could in the presence of the popular star. "She's pretty enough, but she seems to prefer boys. She wouldn't give me a second glance unless I stripped off my gown and flapped my dick in front of her face."

"Something tells me you won't have the same problem with our friend, Olga," Jade laughed. "I caught her glancing in your direction more than once when the spotlight wasn't on her."

"Oh my God," I gushed. "This evening just keeps getting better. This better not be another fairy tale you're pulling over me–"

"I wouldn't *dream* of it," Jade said as she rose up from her seat and caught the attention of one of the passing attendants. "This meeting is very much for real..."

4

Jade whispered something into the ear of the usher, then we waited for the crowd to begin filtering out of the theater after the curtain finally closed.

"So what happens now?" I said, glancing at her with a thumping heart.

"We'll give Olga a few minutes to return to her dressing room, then the usher will escort us backstage to meet her."

"Shouldn't we bring a gift or some flowers or something?" I said.

"Already taken care of," Jade nodded, motioning toward one of the attendants as he walked toward us with a huge bouquet of red roses in his arms.

"Oh my God," I gushed as he handed me the bouquet. "You're spoiling me way more than I deserve tonight."

"Nonsense," Jade smiled, clasping my hand and squeezing it tightly. "You can make it up to me later tonight if you're still in the mood."

"Oh, I'm in the mood alright," I grinned, sliding my finger on the underside of her bare wrist. "All those grand jetés and bulging tights have stimulated a lot more than just my imagination."

"Good," Jade said as the usher indicated for us to follow him through a side door next to the stage. "But try to keep your prick in your pants at least until after you've met Olga. I haven't told her about your special endowments, and seeing your tool slip out the side of your dress might be a bit much for a first impression."

"No worries," I laughed. "I've got enough packaging down there to put a *chastity belt* to shame."

We walked through the maze of corridors at the rear of the theater until the attendant paused outside a closed door marked with Olga's name. He tapped softly on the front of the door and a woman's voice cheerily replied *enter*. When he opened the door, the pretty ballerina sat in front of her mirror, slowly unraveling her French twist updo. When she saw Jade enter the room, she stood up with a big smile, giving her a warm hug and two kisses on the cheek.

"Jade!" she said. "It's so good to see you again. How long has it been? It seems like ages—"

"You've been pretty busy," Jade nodded. "I've been following your tour around the country. I couldn't miss it when it finally came back to our hometown."

"*Adopted* town," Olga chuckled. "You can take the girl out of Russia, but not the Russian influence out of the girl."

"That's what makes you all the more endearing," Jade smiled, turning toward me. "This is my friend Shae, that I was telling you about."

"Yes," Olga said, kissing me gently on the sides of both

cheeks. "Happy thirtieth birthday. You barely look older than a *teenager*."

"Thank you," I smiled, flushing deeply as I handed Olga the large bouquet. "These are for you. I enjoyed your performance tremendously."

"So it would seem," Olga said, noticing the dried tear tracks on the sides of my face and my upper bosom. "Let me help you with that."

She reached down to the front of her makeup desk and picked up a powder puff, lightly dusting it over my cheeks and plunging cleavage while I heaved my chest in excitement.

"There," she said, throwing the sponge back onto her table. "That's much more befitting of a woman in the prime of her life."

"This has certainly been the highlight so far," I gushed. "This is my first ballet, and it took my breath away. Thank you so much for helping Jade secure such wonderful seats."

"It was my pleasure," Olga said. "You shone like a jewel from the front row. I think almost as many people were watching *you* as the performers on the stage."

"I suspect they were staring at someone *else*, sitting not so far away," I chuckled. "It's not very often that you get to rub shoulders with the leading pop artist of our generation."

Olga nodded for a moment while she darted her eyes back and forth between Jade and me.

"Were you able to talk with Taylor during the intermission? I could make an introduction for you if you'd like to meet her..."

"Unfortunately," I said. "She's accompanied by an old friend of mine who's carrying a little extra baggage. I think it's best I avoid any further contact with him for the time being–"

"I know the feeling," Olga laughed. "I've had my share of overbearing boyfriends too. Now I save all my fawning for men for the *stage* only."

"Well, you certainly had *me* convinced," I said. "I haven't cried so hard since I first watched The Notebook."

"That's your favorite movie, *too*?" Olga said, grabbing both of my hands excitedly. "Ryan Gosling was my first movie star crush, though I've subsequently switched sides."

"Yeah," I nodded. "Rachel McAdams is pretty hot. I liked her even more playing opposite Rachael Weisz in the film Disobedience."

"Mmm," Olga hummed. "That was a delicious sex scene."

"Maybe I should leave you two alone for a little while," Jade chuckled, backing toward the front of the dressing room door.

"I'm sorry, baby," Olga said, turning toward Jade and running her hand through her hair. "You didn't tell me your friend was so gorgeous. Why don't the three of us meet for coffee later this week? I'm free on Wednesday or Thursday between rehearsals."

"I'd like that very much," Jade nodded. "I'll send you a text and we can choose a convenient time and place. Congrats on another bravura performance. You slayed it out there, like always."

"Thanks, J," Olga said, kissing Jade on both cheeks, then repeating the gesture with me. "I'm looking forward to seeing both of you again. Keep the faith..."

After Jade and I left Olga's dressing room and exited the theater, we flagged a cab and climbed in the back seat together while we headed back to my place.

"Are you still up for a little nightcap?" Jade smiled, sliding a palm between my still quivering legs.

"I'll need more than a *nightcap* to calm down," I nodded, kissing her hard on the lips as I squeezed her breast tightly. "I haven't been this worked up since—"

"Since Noah left Allie in The Notebook?" Jade chuckled, feeling the swelling in my crotch."

"Since Odette left Siegfried in Swan Lake," I laughed, thrusting my tongue into her mouth. "I'm glad Olga seems to prefer girls now. Maybe you should have told her about my special feature after all."

"Something tells me she'll find out soon enough," Jade said, stretching my tight panties to the side and wrapping her fist around my hardening pole. I haven't seen her respond to another woman so passionately since—"

"Since you copped a feel during sleepover night in junior high?"

"Something like that..." Jade smiled as she slipped her little finger into my dripping hole.

5

———————

Two days after attending the ballet performance, I received a surprise text message from Olga.

Hi Shae, it read. *I got your number from Jade. Would you like to join me for one of my rehearsals? We're gearing up for a holiday performance of The Nutcracker, and I thought you might like to see what goes on behind the scenes...*

I flared my eyes when I glanced at the screen, not expecting the pretty ballerina to contact me before our planned coffee date with Jade. I felt my heart pounding in my chest as I held my fingers over the keyboard, unsure exactly how to reply.

That sounds very exciting, I said, resisting the temptation to add an exclamation mark. *What day were you thinking?*

Are you free tomorrow morning around ten? The rehearsal doesn't start until noon, but I need to warm up beforehand, where we can chat for a bit. Bring something comfortable if you feel like stretching with me.

Stretching with her? I thought to myself. I couldn't believe she was inviting me into her private world after such a brief meeting. The thought of seeing her magnificent body up close and personal caused an immediate stirring in my loins as my cock poked up under my tenting robe.

Definitely, I typed back. *Where will I meet you?*

10 E Randolph Street, 3rd floor. Ring the buzzer at the door and I'll come out to meet you.

Thank you for the invitation, I said. *See you then.*

I hesitated, deciding whether to include the little kiss emoji at the end of my message, opting instead for the flushed-cheeks emoji so as not to come on too strong to her invitation. I was thrilled beyond words to see that she was interested in seeing me privately, but I wasn't sure if this was still just a favor for a friend or genuine interest in exploring something deeper. Either way, there was no way I was going to pass up an opportunity to spend more time with her, especially when I had her all to myself.

I barely slept that night while I imagined myself stretching next to her, staring at her sexy body as she flexed and parted her legs in her tights. The more I thought about it, the harder my cock grew, until I finally had to rub out a quick one so I could settle down and get some rest. But the following morning, while I was contemplating what to wear, I didn't trust myself to keep my dick under control in the two-piece leotard I normally wore to yoga class. So I threw some loose sweats in my gym bag and pulled on my skinny jeans and some sneakers before heading off to her studio downtown.

When I got to her building, I parked in a nearby lot, then took the elevator to the third floor, where two locked glass-panel doors displayed an inscription for the Joffrey Ballet. I noticed a small button beside the door and pressed it, waiting for a reply. About twenty seconds later, Olga's familiar voice came over the small speaker next to the button.

"Shae?" she said in a bright tone.

"Yes–" I answered, followed by a quick buzzer as the lock on the door clicked to signal it was open. Just as I swung it open, Olga rounded the corner from one of the adjacent halls with a broad smile.

"Glad you could make it," she said, skipping toward me wearing a form-fitting leotard and ballet shoes.

She kissed me on the sides of both cheeks in her customary manner, then clasped my hand as she peered happily into my eyes.

"Did you have any trouble finding the place?" she said.

"No," I smiled. "Google Maps is a godsend."

"We've got a couple of hours before I need to join the rest of the group," she said, peering at my tight jeans and curvy sweater. "Did you bring some stretching clothes?"

"Yes," I said, shaking my gym bag in my right hand.

"Good," she said, pulling me gently back in the direction she came from. "We've got a comfortable room where we can have some privacy. You can change in there."

I felt my heart beating again in my chest while I followed her perfect ass down the narrow hall, where she opened a side door leading into a room with hardwood floors and mirrors on both sides, with a brass rail at waist height positioned on the wall.

"You can hang your street clothes on the hook on the far wall," Olga said, closing the door quietly behind us.

"You want me to change *here*?" I said, wrinkling my fore-head at the unusual protocol.

"Of course," Olga smiled. "It's just us girls. We don't want to disturb the rest of the group in the dressing area."

"Okay," I said, placing my gym bag next to the wall and pulling off my sweater to reveal my sports bra underneath. Then I kicked off my sneakers and yanked down my jeans, quickly pulling my sweat pants over my Spanks underwear so Olga wouldn't notice the bulge in my crotch.

"Do you always wear *sweats* when you workout?" Olga said, squinting her eyes at me curiously.

"Only when I'm stretching," I said. "I feel a bit self-conscious with all the prying eyes at the gym. Sometimes I think the only reason guys go to the aerobics and yoga classes is to check out the other girls."

"Probably," Olga laughed. "But you don't have to worry about that here. It will just be the two of us."

"Great," I said, glancing down at my shoes lying on the floor. "Sneakers or bare feet?"

"Bare feet, definitely," Olga nodded. "The less outerwear, the better."

"But you're wearing ballet shoes–"

"Sometimes I need to practice the *en pointe* position, and these shoes give me the extra support I need. But that might be a little too advanced for our first practice session together."

"I would imagine," I chuckled. "What would you like to do first?"

"Why don't we start with some simple stretching exercises?" Olga said, turning toward the mirror and raising one leg, placing her heel over the top of the rail. "This is what we call the *barre* position."

I stood a few feet away from Olga and mimicked her technique, grunting slightly while I raised my leg.

"You've got some pretty good flexibility for an amateur," she nodded, peering down at my ass in my loose sweat pants.

"It must be all those yoga classes," I nodded, not quite ready to tell her about my recent tryst in the truck stop boys' room, where I used my flexibility to maximum advantage next to the glory hole.

"Let's see if you can push it a little further," she said, lowering her torso down on top of her raised leg without the slightest of effort.

I tried to follow her lead, but the tightness in my hamstring muscle restricted my movement as I curled my spine, trying to touch my head to my knee.

"Go slow at first," Olga said, noticing my discomfort. "The trick is to go only far enough until it starts to pinch. Then you need to hold it in that position while you breathe deeply until you feel your muscles begin to relax. With practice, you can bend your body in almost limitless ways."

"So it appears," I smiled, stealing a glance between her separated legs, noticing the shape of a camel toe in the crotch of her tights.

"Are you ready to try something *else*?" she said, seeing the sweat forming above my brow.

"Definitely," I said, dreaming about my hard cock in her sexy snatch.

"Let's try the *arabesque position* next," Olga said, pulling her leg off the bar and turning to face in the opposite direction.

She lifted the same leg backwards in a perfect arc while keeping her torso upright, then she placed her pointed toes over the bar with her hands extended gracefully in front of her to counterbalance her weight.

I attempted to mimic her form but felt myself tipping unsteadily while I tried to keep myself balanced on one foot. Olga lowered her leg and positioned her body next to mine, then she placed one hand under my raised thigh and the other under my heaving chest.

"This one's a little tougher to keep your balance," she said. "Let me help you find the right position..."

As she pulled my leg slightly upward, I could feel her fingers probing close to my swelling organ and my tingling breasts, hoping that she wouldn't detect my swelling cock that betrayed my growing interest in her as more than a stretching partner.

"Try to raise your chest a little higher and extend your arms in the same line as your extended leg," she said while pressing her palm just below my breasts.

"Is this better?" I said, turning my head to glance at her firm breasts in her tight leotard, positioned precisely at face height.

"Yes, but try to keep your head facing forward to maintain the correct line. In ballet, it's all about proper body alignment."

"I'm trying," I panted. "But it's not so easy when I have a hot dancer standing next to me."

"Okay, let's try something different then," Olga said, pulling my leg down from the bar and sliding her other hand down the side of my torso as I turned around to face her. "Sometimes I also need to stretch my adductor muscles to perform the *saut de chat* jump..."

"I'm not familiar with that one–" I said, darting my eyebrows.

"It's when you leap into the air with your legs spread apart horizontally, as opposed to *en jeté,* when you extend them forward and back."

"Oh yes, it's so graceful when you perform that on the stage."

"That's because I practice my ass off in rehearsal," Olga laughed. "Come, let me show you how."

She sat down on the floor with her back toward the

mirror, then she straightened her legs out in front of her and angled them apart ninety degrees, bending her torso forward until her chest lay softly on the floor between her split legs. I positioned myself facing her and tried to follow her lead, but was only able to spread my legs about sixty degrees apart and lower my torso halfway to the floor.

"It's easier when you have a little *help*," she said, raising her body and shuffling her hips forward a few inches until the soles of our feet touched. Then she held out her hands and smiled at me while I used every ounce of my willpower not to stare between her split legs at her perfect ass and tight pussy, barely concealed by her skin-tight leotard.

"Hold my hands while I pull you toward me," she said. "You'll feel a little pressure on the insides of your thighs, so tell me when it begins to pinch, so I can hold you in the right position."

As she pulled my torso toward her and my face lowered nearer to her crotch while she spread my feet slowly apart, I gasped when I noticed a small wet spot forming in the middle of her slit.

"Too *hard*?" she said, easing up on her grip while she relaxed the pressure on my protesting muscles.

"*Something's* getting hard," I blurted out as I felt my swelling dick pressing against the front of my tight underwear. "This is stimulating in more ways than I anticipated–"

"This one is pretty sexy," Olga nodded, staring at the loose folds of my sweats covering my straining crotch. "But not as sexy when you're wearing sweatpants."

I paused for a moment, unsure she was thinking the same thing I was.

"I only have underwear underneath–' I said, trying to give her advance warning.

"That's alright," Olga smiled. "It's just us two girls in here. I won't tell if you don't."

"Olga," I said, peering at her straight in the eye while my hands trembled in her fingers. "There's something I haven't yet told you about me. I'm not sure it's a good idea to take off any more of my clothes..."

"Why?" she said, staring at the crotch of my pants. "Are you hiding something dangerous down there?"

"In a manner of speaking–"

"I promise not to judge," Olga smiled. "This isn't the first time I've been with a girl, you know."

"Well, I'm a special type of girl..."

"You certainly are," Olga said, bending her knees and shuffling her hips forward until she pressed her wet crotch against the front of my swelling underwear. When she threaded her legs around the back of my ass and wrapped her arms around my neck, pulling our bodies closer together, her eyes flared when she felt the hard bulge in my pants.

"Oh my God," she said, pulling her head back suddenly. "Are you a–?"

"I'm a *girl*," I said, trying to allay her worst fear. "Just a girl with a little extra *surprise*."

"You mean like a–?"

"Not a transexual in the regular way," I said, contorting my face into an uncomfortable grimace. "I was *born* intersex."

"How do you mean?" Olga said, sliding her palms down the center of my back, under the band of my sports bra.

"I've got two X chromosomes and look like a woman in every *other* way. I was just born with a man's penis in place of a clitoris."

"You mean you have a *vagina* also?" she said, widening her eyes.

"Yes, and real breasts, not fake ones–"

"I noticed those right away," she smiled. sliding her hands around the side of my back and squeezing my tits softly over my bra. "I can tell from their teardrop shape and the softness of your flesh."

"And my nipples," I sighed, pulling her hands under the bottom of my bra and pinching her fingers over my swelling bullets. "There are no stitches or artificial padding under there, either."

"Mmm," Olga hummed, drawing her face closer to mine and kissing me sexily around the edges of my lips. "So I can see..."

"Are you sure you want to do this?" I said, glancing toward the closed door. "Are we safe in here alone?"

"I locked the door right after we entered,' Olga nodded as she pressed her hand under the waistband of my sweatpants. "I'm way ahead of you, girl."

As she squeezed her fingers under my underwear and flipped my semi-tumescent cock upwards to release the strain in my pants, I smiled at her while I thrust my tongue into her mouth, rubbing my hard-on against her wet crotch as I moaned in her mouth.

I wonder if they have a name for this ballet maneuver, I thought to myself as Olga pulled my sweats pants down over my knees.

6

W hen Olga saw my huge erection straining against my tight underwear, she pulled down my Spanx leggings and flared her eyes when my hard-on popped up.

"Oh my God," she panted, staring at my dripping crown and glistening vulva. "You weren't kidding when you said you were a special kind of girl."

"Is it too much?" I said, noticing her surprised expression. "Does it turn you off?"

"Quite the opposite," she said, wrapping her hand around my shaft and squeezing it tightly. "This is possibly the sexiest thing I've ever seen..."

"Even though you said you *switched sides*? You don't mind being with a girl who has a *cock*?"

"Well, I've tried *strap-ons* before," she smiled. "This one's just a little more real than the ones I'm accustomed to using."

"I'll be happy to oblige," I grinned. "If you still feel in the mood–"

"I am now," Olga said, shifting her hips forward while she rubbed my upturned erection against her wet tights.

I kissed her hard on her lips, then reached down to pull her leotard aside, pointing the tip of my pole toward her opening. She raised herself and angled her hips forward, pressing my prick inside her while we moaned in each other's mouths.

"Oh my God, Shae," Olga groaned when she felt me filling her up. "I had no idea..."

"Really?" I said. "Jade didn't mention anything to you?"

"No, she just said you two were special friends."

"Apparently, there was some history between the two of *you* also," I smiled as I peered at her flushed face.

"We had a little dalliance back in the day," Olga nodded. "But that was innocent flirting between girls. Nothing as hard-core as this."

"Oh?" I said, pressing the base of my dick harder against her dripping pussy. "Are you enjoying *my* hard core?"

"Fuck, yes," Olga growled, wrapping her legs around the back of my ass. "Fuck me harder. I want to feel you coming inside me."

"Are you getting close?" I said. "Because I want to feel you coming with me."

"Yes," she said, squeezing my tits harder in her hands. "I'm going to come like I've never come before–"

"Oh fuck, Olga," I hissed, feeling my body pass over the point of no return as my dick started to pulse in her pussy. "I can't hold it any longer–"

"Yes, baby," Olga groaned, interlocking her feet behind my butt and squeezing my hips hard. *"Nnguhhh!"*

When I felt her gushing on my dripping pussy, I pulled her closer to me as the two of us shook violently in each other's arms. We held onto each other for what seemed like an eternity, while successive waves of passion engulfed the two of us in a long, powerful climax. But just as we jerked our bodies together in one final, strong contraction, a loud tap suddenly came from the other side of the door.

"Olga?" a man's voice called as the doorknob rattled loudly. "Are you in there? Rehearsal is about to begin, and the rest of the company is waiting for you."

"Yes, Ashley," Olga called back. "I'm just finishing my warm-up. I'll be there in a minute."

When we heard the footfalls stomping off down the hall, Olga raised her eyebrows at me, giggling softly.

"Have I gotten you into trouble?" I said, wrinkling my brow in concern.

"Only the best *kind* of trouble," she grinned, kissing me softly while she pressed our breasts together. "But I should probably get going, so I don't keep the rest of the group waiting. Do you want to watch me from the wings after you get dressed?"

"Really?" I said, flaring my eyes open in surprise. "Your boss won't mind if I spy on your rehearsal?"

"Just stay in the shadows and out of the way of the dancers," she nodded. "If he mentions anything, I'll tell him you're here on my invitation."

Olga pulled her hips away from me, then she glanced down at the mess we'd made on the floor, squinting her eyes in dismay.

"Do you mind if I use your underwear to clean myself up?" she said. "I can't go out there in my present condition."

"No worries," I smiled, handing her my Spanx undergarment. "I won't be needing it now anyhow. I was only wearing it so you wouldn't notice my swelling erection."

"Well, it's certainly got my attention *now*," she grinned, flapping my pole softly from side to side while she watched my cum dripping down the side of my shaft. "You better use this to clean yourself up, too."

While I wiped the residual cum off my dripping tool, Olga stood up and readjusted her leotard, turning around to appraise herself in the mirror.

"It's a good thing you pulled my tights to the side before we went much further," she laughed. "Otherwise, I would have created a giant wet spot in the crotch of my tights. Do I look ready to go out in public?"

"You'd look beautiful in a *potato sack*," I smiled, glancing at her beautiful ass in her tight leotard. "But if you're asking if everything looks presentable after our little tryst, it's a yes."

"Alright then," Olga said, sliding her palms over her wrinkled uniform and lifting her breasts back into position. "Come join me after you've gotten yourself put back together. Our studio is the third door at the end of the hall."

"It might take a minute or two to dampen my excitement," I chuckled, glancing down at my flapping erection, still bobbing against the front of my stomach. "I'm still pretty worked up about fucking the woman of my dreams."

"Me too," Olga said, heading toward the door and peering outside to make sure nobody was idling nearby. "I'll be keeping that thought while I perform my jetés and pas de deux. Now have even more incentive to spread my legs apart while I'm leaping for joy."

"I can't wait," I smiled, staring at her pretty ass as she closed the door behind her. "I'll try to keep things contained while I watch you from a distance."

As Olga closed the door softly behind her, I glanced in

the mirror at my upturned erection, still throbbing in excitement from the unexpected encounter we'd both shared.

Now that's a performance I won't soon forget, I grinned, stumbling to my feet as a long string of cum swung from the end of my throbbing organ.

7

———

I t took a few minutes for my dick to return to its semi-flaccid state, then I pulled on my jeans and tucked it between my wet folds, placing the soiled underwear in my gym bag. When I thought it was safe to go back out in public, I opened the door and headed down the hall in the direction of the practice studio. As I neared the end of the corridor, I heard symphony music emanating from behind a closed door, and when I swung it open, I saw a group of dancers flitting around a makeshift stage. Olga was positioned in the center of the group, and when I saw her, I retreated quietly to the side of the room, next to an assembly of Christmas props.

Olga didn't seem to notice me while she performed her maneuvers, which was to be expected, given the frequent interruptions of the artistic director. After every scene, he would offer instruction to the dancers, including Olga, who seemed to be the focus of his critical feedback.

"We need to tighten up the toy soldier scene," he barked to the dancers. "You're not keeping a fixed distance between your partners. Dmitri, you keep losing your mark on the floor when you spin in place, and Denis, the line of your arms is not in sync with the others. And Olga, what's going on with your leaps today? They're not as high as I'm accustomed, and your leg extension is listless and lethargic."

"It's nothing, Ashley," Olga said, glancing at me out of the sides of her eyes. "I'm just feeling a little tired today. I'll have more energy when we go live."

"It's your job to be perfect *every* day, including rehearsal days," the director said, furling his eyebrows. "This is why we have understudies. Do you want to sit out the next scene while Kira takes your place?"

"No," Olga said, shuffling her feet in frustration. "I'll be fine. Don't take me out."

"Alright then," the director said, crossing his arms. "Let's run it again, and this time, perform it like you *mean* it. I don't want any more slouching or stumbling."

The dancers took up their positions again, and when the music restarted, they glided together in unison, kicking their heels and spinning their tight bodies in a whirlwind of motion. For the life of me, I couldn't detect a single flaw in anyone's form as they flexed their legs and waved their arms in perfect synchronicity. When it was Olga's turn to join the routine, her spins and leaps looked perfect, except for a thin wet spot in the crotch of her tights when she did the splits. I wasn't sure if she was aware of the blemish, and I wanted to warn her as the director squinted his eyes in her direction, but she never looked at me, and began to wonder if she was angry with me for distracting her during the pre-rehearsal warm-up.

After a long and exhausting practice session, the director finally called it a wrap, and the dancers shuffled toward the dressing room to change and head home for the day. When Olga saw me waiting next to the Christmas tree, she paused by my side, clasping my hand softly.

"Sorry about that," she said. "You must find all of this intolerably boring."

"Not at all," I smiled. "It's fascinating to watch your group's process and the director's instruction. I had no idea there were so many elements to balance and synchronize as a team."

"Yeah," Olga nodded. "Ashley can be a bit of a ball-buster. But he sees things we often don't when we're performing. I suppose that's his job..."

"Are you sure you weren't distracted with me standing in the wings?"I said. "I'd hate to be the one responsible for taking your edge off–"

"You took the edge off alright," she grinned. "But in the best possible way. I couldn't stop thinking about you *inside* me all the time I was out there."

"I wondered if your head wasn't fully in the game," I chuckled. "Did you realize you're still wet in the crotch of your tights?"

Olga stepped a few feet beside me and peered at herself in the mirror lining the wall, then she shook her head in dismay.

"It looks like I didn't clean up as well as I thought," she grimaced. "Hopefully, it just looked like *sweat* instead of something else."

"I won't tell if you don't," I said, resisting the temptation to squeeze her tight ass.

She turned her head while she watched the last of the dancers following the artistic director out of the room, then she kissed me gently on the cheek.

"Why don't you wait for me in the lobby while I get

changed? Do you feel like something to eat? I can whip something up at my place if you're hungry."

"I'm *hungry* alright," I nodded. "But not for food. I've been dreaming about eating something *else* for the last two hours."

"Me too," Olga grinned. "Let's get out of this place and get back to where we left off. There's a million other things I want to do to you before we separate again."

"Who says we have to *separate*?" I smiled. "I can think of plenty of ways we can stay connected while we explore the possibilities."

"Save that thought," Olga smiled as she cupped her hand between my thighs and squeezed my throbbing organ. "Because I plan on exploring *all* of the possibilities..."

8

———

We drove back to Olga's place in my car, and during the ride, I asked her about her upcoming performance.

"So The Nutcracker is a Christmas-themed ballet?" I said, remembering the props I saw in the practice studio.

"Yes," she nodded. "It's very light and cheerful, unlike the ominous tone of Swan Lake."

"When will you be performing your first live production?"

"The first show in Chicago is at Harris Theater on December 10. Would you like to go?"

"Of course!" I said. "I want to see everything you do. You had me smitten from the moment I first saw you."

"You want to see *everything*?" Olga smiled, reaching over to caress the inside of my thigh. "Are you sure about that?"

"Definitely. I've only known you for a few days so far. I feel like I'm just beginning to scratch the surface of what you've got to offer."

"Well, you've certainly penetrated more than just the

outside layer," she laughed, sliding her fingers softly over the growing bulge in my crotch.

"Can I ask you something?" I said, squinting at the GPS display as we pulled into her condo building's underground garage.

"Of course. You can ask me anything."

"I noticed when you were practicing your routine in the studio with the rest of the troupe that you never looked at me. Was that because you were concentrating on your moves, or are you never allowed to look at the audience?"

Olga laughed as she pointed toward her designated parking space and she pulled her keys out of her purse.

"Technically, we're only supposed to look at the characters we're interacting with on the stage, but in this instance, the main reason was because I knew that if I looked at you, I wouldn't be able to maintain my composure. It took everything in my power as it *was* to finish the practice without jumping your bones."

"Whew," I sighed in relief as we walked toward the elevator lobby. "I thought maybe you were angry with me for sapping all your energy beforehand in the stretching room."

"Well, you *did* sap most of my energy, but in a good way," she smiled. "That was one of the strongest orgasms I've had in a long time."

When we got into the elevator and the door slid closed, Olga tapped the button for the twenty-third floor, then she turned around to face me, raising one of her legs over the side of my hips and grinding her crotch against me. By the time we reached her floor, my dick was straining against my tight jeans, begging for some breathing room. When we stumbled into her apartment, we began kissing passionately while we tried to pull off each other's clothes, falling onto the nearest soft piece of furniture as we intertwined our bodies.

"Jesus, Shae," Olga panted as she lowered her face down the front of my trembling body toward my raging erection. "You're the sexiest woman I've ever been with–"

"Is that only because I've got larger *love muscle* than the rest of them?" I chuckled as she paused her head over the tip of my bobbing organ.

"Slightly?" she said, flaring her eyes as she gawked at my dripping hard-on. "I've had enough liaisons with men to know you're endowed far better than just about anybody, male or female. Do you mind sitting up for a moment so I can admire your entire body?"

"Sure," I said, happy to show off my endowments while she rolled her body off the sofa and knelt on the floor between my parted knees.

"Oh my God," she gushed, pulling her head back a few inches to appraise my entire perineum. "It's a veritable work of art. Between your perfectly straight, enormous phallus and your pretty, glistening folds, you look like a Georgia O'Keefe painting..."

"Albeit one with a larger *pistil* than most," I chuckled.

"And what a magnificent pistil it is," she said, sliding her fingertips down the side of my throbbing shaft toward my dripping vulva. She paused at the junction of my folds, watching my pussy spasming from her delicate touch. "Does it feel good when I touch you *here*, too?"

"Yes," I panted, tilting my head downward while I watched her explore my sex. "The doctors told me my cock is really just an extension of my clitoris, which extends further inside my pussy, like every other woman's..."

"So you like to be probed inside, too?" Olga said, sliding her index and middle finger slowly into my slit.

"Yes," I moaned while I flitted my eyes open and shut in pleasure.

"What about *here*?" she said, curling her fingers upward in a come-hither motion as she peered at my glazed pupils.

"Definitely," I groaned, tilting my hips to press her fingers harder against the upper surface of my cavern. "I've got a G-spot just like any other girl."

"Does it make you *gush* like other girls, too?" she smiled, watching my erection bobbing between my legs as a thick drop of pre-cum slid out the tip.

"Yes, in more ways than one," I grunted.

"I'd like to see that," Olga grinned as she pressed the base of her hand hard against my dripping slit. "Last time, I could only *feel* you coming inside me. This time, I want to *watch* when I make you climax."

"It won't take much longer if you keep stimulating me like *that*," I huffed, staring at the ruddy color of my organ deepening as my pleasure spread around my entire pelvic area.

"Maybe you'll like it even more if I stimulate you in *both* places at the same time," Olga nodded, removing her slippery fingers from my pussy and rolling them around my sensitive crown while she inserted her other hand in the front entrance of my dripping slit.

"God, yes," I groaned, throwing my head against the back of the sofa as my dick pulsed in her hands, sending a waterfall of precum streaming down over her fingers.

"Mmm," she smiled as she watched my face flushing and my nipples hardening on my heaving chest as she pumped my dick harder and curled her fingers against my tingling G-spot. "What a sight you are to behold. This is like my very own stage performance that I get to enjoy from the other side of the aisle, complete with its own props and rousing soundtrack..."

"Yes, Olga," I grunted as I watched her stroking my organs with both hands. "I'm going to come soon. I can feel it getting close to the bursting point–"

"Let it go, baby," Olga nodded, gaping her mouth open over the tip of my swelling glans. "I want to watch you squirting all over my face and my tits when you come. You're driving me crazy with desire."

When I glanced down at her firm tits shaking while she rocked her body against mine and saw the stream of juices running down the insides of her thighs, I groaned loudly when I felt the floodgates open and my pussy and dick pulsed at the same time, ejecting successive waves of spunk and pussy juice all over her blinking face and heaving chest while she gulped down my cum. It was a glorious sight, watching her worshipping my entire perineum while she held my cock tightly in one hand and pressed the fingers of her other against my flexing opening as she smiled up at my jerking head. I don't think I'd come so hard or so long in my entire life, and by the time I finally finished shaking and contracting in delirious ecstasy, I glanced down at her body, noticing just how much I'd squirted and sprayed all over her naked figure. Her cheeks and her shoulders were covered in long streaks of cum, and her tits were glistening in a thick glaze of pussy juice, covering virtually the entire front half of her torso.

"Holy fuck!" Olga said, pulling away from my bobbing organ as she gently retracted her fingers from my dripping pussy. "That was the sexiest thing I've ever done, with either a man or a woman!"

"I guess you got two for the price of one this time," I

smiled. "I suppose that's why some people call me a *ladyboy*."

"Well, you're a lot more *lady* than boy as far as I'm concerned," Olga smiled as she licked the dribbling semen from the underside of my crown. "Just one with a prettier and bigger *sex* organ than most. I can't wait to feel you coming in my mouth next time. Do you need a little extra time to recover, or can I enjoy the *rest* of my meal before lunchtime is over?"

"I think it's time we switched places for a while," I grinned, leaning forward to kiss her lips and taste my cum in her mouth. "You're not the only one who's hungry for a little dessert."

"You're twisting my arm, girl," Shae grinned as she twisted my hard nipples with her fingers. "Maybe just for a short interlude. Because I've got some ideas for our final act that will blow the audience away."

"I'll look forward to that," I smiled, sliding my body off the front of the sofa and wrapping my legs around the back of her ass while pressing my throbbing hard-on between her dripping thighs. "But not before we ramp up the tension a little further in the middle section of the performance..."

"You seem to be learning the plotlines of my plays more quickly than most," Olga laughed as I slid my hands around the front of her torso and pressed her body harder against the seat cushions of the sofa.

"Those aren't the *only* lines of your performance that I'm beginning to learn," I grinned as I tilted my hips upward and sunk my dick deep into her burning hole. "Let me see if I can scratch your itch somewhere differently this time..."

9

"**O**h God, Shae," Olga groaned when she felt me entering her from behind. "You feel so good inside me."

"You have no idea how much I've dreamed about fucking this ass of yours since I saw you performing on the stage," I grunted.

"In *Swan Lake*, you mean?" she said.

"Yes, your figure is every woman's dream.'

"*Sex* dream or *body* dream?"

"Both," I huffed, slapping my mound against her tight cheeks.

"What about *men*?" she laughed.

"I'm sure just as many of them were dreaming about fucking you, too," I chuckled. "Probably *more*."

"What about you?" she said while she grasped the edge of the sofa to support her rocking body. "Weren't you attracted to the sexy men in tights?"

"I was until you showed up," I smiled, reaching around the side of her back to squeeze her firm t_ts. "At that point, an entirely new part of my body started tingling..."

Olga paused her hip movement for a moment while she peered over her shoulder at my flushed cheeks.

"Have you been with men before?" she said. "I mean, *sexually*?"

"Yes," I said, peering at her with a wrinkled forehead. "But can we continue this conversation after we're *finished*?"

"I suppose so," she chuckled. "I'm just interested to know how versatile you are."

"Let's just say *plenty*," I smiled. "I believe I was given two sets of sex organs for a reason. I plan on taking maximum advantage of both of them as long as I can."

"I'd like to see that sometime," Olga nodded, reaching between her thighs to squeeze the base of my hard-on while it throbbed inside her pussy. "There's something about the thought of two guys doing it that I find insanely arousing."

"But I'm not a guy–"

"All the more exciting to watch," she said. "You're a beautiful woman with a well-endowed cock. I can't imagine anything sexier than to see you getting it on with a buff, handsome dude."

"You should have seen me *two weeks* ago," I chuckled, reflecting back on my unusual liaison with the truckers at the glory hole men's room.

"Why?" Olga said, starting to rock her hips again against my throbbing erection. "What happened *then*?"

I hesitated for a moment, watching my dick sliding in and out of her pink pussy, then I smiled, realizing that the more we chatted, the more turned on she was becoming.

"I had an unexpected encounter with some men in a truck stop washroom."

Olga paused her humping action again while she glanced over her shoulder at me, raising an eyebrow.

"Do you normally use the *men's* room when you have to go?" she said.

"Not usually. But in this case, the lineup for the ladies' room was a little too long."

"So what happened after you went in there?"

"I went to use one of the cubicles for a little extra privacy, and I was surprised to find a cut-out between the partition wall dividing the two stalls..."

"A *glory hole*, you mean?" Olga said, peering back at me with flaring eyes.

"I suppose you could call it that," I chuckled, squeezing the sides of her ass softly.

"Did you stick your *dick* through it?"

"Not at first," I said. "I just watched the guy getting off in the compartment next to mine. But it didn't take long for things to start ramping up..."

"What did you do then?" she said, becoming increasingly interested in my story.

"He stuck his cock through the hole and I sucked him off, then he did the same to me."

"Holy fuck!" Olga grunted, sinking my hard-on deeper inside her burning pussy. "That's insane. Did you both *come*?"

"Of course," I laughed, slapping her ass playfully.

"What was that like?" she said. "I mean, having sex with an anonymous stranger in a public washroom?"

"A lot sexier than I would have imagined," I laughed. "I don't know if it was the sense of danger doing it in a public place, or the fact that neither of us could see each other the whole time, but either way, it was the dirtiest and sexiest thing I'd done up to that point in my life."

"You never even looked at the guy on the other side of the partition?" she said, squinting at me.

"Not at first. But it didn't take long for the other guys using the restroom to hear what was going on behind the closed doors, and after a while, a bit of a lineup began to form outside my compartment door from men wanting their turn with me. After a while, I dispensed with the artifice of using the hole in the wall to connect our bodies together, and I serviced them one at a time right there in my own cubicle."

"Jesus," Olga grunted as she humped her hips faster against my tingling erection. "What kind of things did you do with them once you had easier access?"

"Just about *everything*," I said, squeezing her ass harder while I watched my pole driving in and out of her cheeks. "They fucked me, then I fucked *them*, then I tried it with two guys–"

"Two guys?!" Olga said, stopping her rocking action again while she peered at me over her shoulder. "How is that even *possible*?"

"Plenty of ways," I smiled, thrusting my dick against her butt to get her back in the rhythm of fucking. "I've got more than one *hole*, you know. But my favorite way is to put both of their dicks in my pussy at the same time..."

"DP?" Olga shuddered as her fingers curled tighter over the cushions of the sofa while her face flushed a deep shade of pink. "This is getting hotter by the moment–"

"Oh?" I moaned, feeling the pleasure in my hips building to the bursting point. "Does it turn you on to imagine me fucking two guys at the same time?"

"Fuck, yes," Olga groaned as she tilted her ass upward to angle my pole against her G-spot. "Have you ever fucked a man in the *ass*?"

"A couple of times," I nodded, feeling my pussy starting

to expand inside as it prepared to clamp down with strong, climactic contractions.

"Fuck me hard, like you do a *man*," Olga hissed, squeezing my shaft with her leaking pussy. "I want to feel you pulsing inside me when you empty your load."

"Yes, Olga," I huffed. "You're driving me crazy. Here it comes. Oh *fuckkkk...*"

"Mmmgahh," Olga hissed, pressing her cheeks hard against my quivering stomach while I held her tightly against me and we both gushed simultaneously over the edge of her leather sofa and the expensive oriental carpet lying on the floor.

It was a glorious feeling, watching her shaking ass while we climaxed together and my hard-on ejected one long, hard jet of cream inside her slippery tunnel. When we both finally stopped shaking and groaning, I collapsed over her heaving back, resting my tits on her sweaty skin.

"Holy *shit*, girl," Olga panted as she stretched her arms off to the side of the sofa. "I'm beginning to feel a bit of *penis envy* from all the different ways you can use your equipment and the different people you can hook up with."

"Well, if you want to *watch* sometime," I smiled, caressing the sides of her breasts gently. "I suppose that could be arranged."

"Actually," she grinned, glancing at me as I lay my head next to hers. "I might know a couple of good candidates. Most of the men in my ballet company are gay."

"That's a shame," I smiled back at her. "Because I was already dreaming of Siegfried fucking me before you entered the picture..."

"I have a feeling that some of my friends would be happy to mix it up with someone with your endowments if you'd let me share your little secret."

"Do you just want to *watch*?" I grinned.

"In this case," she smiled. "I'd be willing to make an exception with my preferred partners. With multiple cocks and two pussies in the mix, I'm sure we could find plenty of ways to share the spoils..."

10

———

I didn't hear from Olga for a few days after our exciting liaison at her apartment, during which time she said she'd try to set a meeting up with some of her colleagues. When I received a text from her later in the week saying she'd scheduled a meet-up at a local coffee shop, I jumped at the chance to see her again, arriving fifteen minutes early, barely able to contain my excitement. When I saw her walk in the front entrance with two other dancers from her company, my heart skipped a beat, recognizing the faces of the two lead soloists from the Swan Lake production.

"Shae!" she smiled when she saw me sitting at a table near the window. "It's great to see you again. I hope you don't mind that I invited a couple of friends to join us today. We needed a little break after another intense practice session at the studio."

"Of course not," I said, standing up to kiss her gently on both sides of her cheek.

"This is Dmitri and Alek," she said, introducing me to

the other dancers. "Perhaps you recognize them from our recent performance at the Lyric Opera House?"

"Of course," I nodded, shaking their hands softly. "*Siegfried and Benno*, right? I couldn't take my eyes off the two of you when you performed your solo routines. You're both so graceful and elegant."

"Tell that to our *artistic director*," Dmitri huffed, shaking his head in frustration. "He seems to find fault in almost everything we do."

"I guess it's his job to find the imperfections that the rest of us don't see," I nodded. "But from my perspective, I think you're both flawless."

The coffee shop waitress stopped by our table to ask what we wanted to drink, and after placing our orders, there was a brief silence while the two men peered at me curiously.

"Olga tells us you're friends," Alek said. "Are you a dancer also?"

"In a manner of speaking," I chuckled. "I perform in a cabaret act at the Lips Revue."

"Isn't that a *female impersonator* show?" Dmitri said, staring at my plump breasts in my tight sweater.

I hesitated for a moment, unsure how to respond to his inquiry, then Olga reached her hand over the table beside me, clasping my fingers gently.

"They're not *all* men," she laughed. "Some of them are just women who are pretending to be men pretending to be women."

"I think I recognize you," Alek said, squinting his eyes at me suspiciously. "I've been to the show a couple of times. It's pretty hot."

"Oh?" I said. "Do you enjoy watching men dressing up like women?"

"It's good fun after all the serious and traditional roles we perform on the ballet stage. I think a lot of people have a certain amount of gender ambivalence. Your dance partners are just brave enough to celebrate it openly."

"Is it gender or *sexual* ambivalence?" Olga said, taking a sip of her coffee. "The two ideas often get confused."

"Technically," I nodded. "*Gender* relates purely to one's sense of male or female identity. Whereas sexual persuasion relates to which gender they prefer to hook up with. Speaking for my dance partners, they still identify as *men* when they're out of costume, though most of them are gay."

"There are a lot of misconceptions in the dance world," Dmitri said, nodding toward Alek. "I suspect most people think that if a man chooses to be a dancer, that he's automatically gay. But in our case, that's only true for *one* of us. Alek appears to be straight all the way."

"But haven't you both experimented from time to time?" Olga said, trying to steer the conversation back to me. "There seems to be a lot more freedom and opportunity in the realm of the arts."

"Not since I was a young man," Alek said. "But I suppose that's true of most people. Society frowns upon boys and girls having sex at a young age, so we're often forced to experiment with our peers."

Olga paused for a moment while she peered at me out of the corner of her eye.

"There's nothing that would tempt you to switch sides again?" she said with a devious smile.

"Not really," Dmitri said. "I can't speak for Alek, but I'm pretty *hard-wired* to have relationships with men only. The thought of having sex with a woman is frankly repulsive to me."

"I'd have to agree in the case of sex with other men," Alek said.

"What if your partner were *intersex*?" Olga said, tapping her foot playfully next to mine under the table. "Having a sexual form and identity of *both* genders?"

"You mean like a ladyboy?" Alek said, wrinkling his forehead.

"Yes," Olga nodded. "What if you saw a man who looked for all intents and purposes like a beautiful woman when she was fully dressed? Wouldn't you still be attracted to her?"

"I suppose if I didn't know what he was packing underneath his clothes. But it would be a major turnoff once I saw her with a dick instead of a pussy–"

"What if she had *both*?" Olga grinned.

"Isn't that impossible?" Dmitri said. "I mean surgically and hormonally, don't you have to be one or the other?"

"Not necessarily," Olga said. "Some people are born with physiological features of both sexes. It's rare, but it happens."

"That would be very–*strange*," Alek said, suddenly shifting uncomfortably in his chair.

"Your body language suggests otherwise," Olga chuckled. "Are you feeling a visceral reaction to the thought?"

"Um–" Alek stammered, clearly unwilling to betray his growing arousal.

"Imagine all the things you could do with someone having both sets of sexual organs," Olga continued. "You could do all the normal things that you do with your preferred gender, but also experiment with all the other stuff you tried with your friends in high school or college. Tell me haven't fantasized about sucking another man's cock or watching him cream over your balls since then."

"Jesus," Alek panted, crossing his legs awkwardly and leaning over the front of the table to conceal the growing bulge in his pants.

"Exactly," Olga grinned. "And what about *you,* Dmitri? What if your partner had a beautiful, huge cock, but just happened to look like a sexy woman everywhere else? Wouldn't you want to play with her big ladyboy cock if you had a chance?"

"I've been with trans boys before," he nodded. "But never one who had both sets of fully functioning equipment."

"Do you find the idea intriguing?" Olga said.

"Yes, but where would you find someone like that? I don't imagine they advertise their unique physiognomy to the average passerby."

Olga paused again for a long moment while she slid her toe up the inside of my calf.

"What would you say if I told you I happen to know someone who has all of these features, and more? Someone who is drop-dead gorgeous, and has a dick that puts every *normal* man's to shame?"

"You've certainly got my attention," Dmitri said, reaching down to adjust his hardening dick in his pants.

"What do you say, Shae?" Olga said, turning toward me with a Cheshire-Cat-sized grin. "Are you willing to try stretching everyone's sexual and gender identities?"

I paused while I darted my eyes between Dmitri and Alek, who peered back at me with shocked looks on their faces.

"You mean–?" Alek said, pinching his brows while he stared at my curvy breasts in my tight, form-fitting sweater.

As a soft blush began to spread over my face, I nodded gently.

"You could have fooled me," Dmitri said, leaning in

closer to detect any sign of an Adam's apple in my throat. "You look one hundred percent like a woman to me."

"Thank you," I smiled. "But not quite *one hundred* percent–"

I pushed my chair back a few inches and turned it partly to the side so they could see my lower half, then I spread my legs slowly apart to reveal my eight-inch pole pressing down the inside of my pant leg.

"Holy *shit!*" Dmitri said, flaring his eyes open when he saw my hard-on in my jeans.

"*Now* do you think you could switch sides if the moment were right?" Olga chuckled, watching both men's reaction to the sight of my throbbing erection in my stretchy jeans.

"With a prick like that," Dmitri chuckled. "I'd be willing to switch sides in more ways than one."

"What about you, Alek?" Olga said, turning toward her other friend. "If Shae were amenable, would you be interested in exploring the other side of your sexual preferences?"

"I'd sure as hell be interested to see what she looks like with her clothes off..." he nodded. "Because I've been undressing her with my eyes practically from the moment we entered the coffee shop."

"Would you like to sip something other than a warm cup of coffee?" Olga smiled. "Because I've got plenty of room back at my place to begin exploring each other's sexual boundaries."

Dmitri, Alek and I darted our eyes between the three of us for a moment, then our faces flushed a deep shade of red while we all thought the same thing.

"I thought so," Olga chuckled, plopping a twenty-dollar-bill on the table and standing up to put on her coat. "Let's get the hell out of here and finish our lunch elsewhere."

"Yes," Alek nodded, standing up with a prominent bulge in his pants. "Suddenly, I've worked up a hell of an appetite."

"Same here," Dmitri said, bunching his coat over the front of his trousers to conceal his upturned erection, pointed off to the side of his pants. "I've got a rumbling in my lower belly that I haven't felt in a long time."

"We better get going, then," Olga smiled as she stared at the bulges in each of our pants. "Before one of your Jack-in-the-boxes blows a top..."

11

———

We drove separately back to Olga's apartment, and after everybody arrived, Olga prepared some coffee in her kitchen while the rest of us sat awkwardly on her sofa, trying not to make eye contact.

"I'm not sure we need any more caffeine after our stimulating discussion at the coffee shop," Olga said, placing a steaming cup in front of each of us. "But at least it will keep our hands occupied until we figure out what to do next."

Dmitri and Alek picked up their mugs and sipped their drinks quietly for a moment, then Alek was the first to break the ice.

"Are there any other women in your cabaret troupe?" he said to me. "I mean, *real* women. That is–"

"It's okay," I laughed. "I know what you mean. All the others are cisgender men, besides me."

"Why did you decide to join a female impersonator group if you identify as female?" Dmitri said, wrinkling his forehead.

"I decided that since I already had some male equipment, plus all the other features of a woman, that I had a bit of a leg up on the other performers. Unlike the others, I don't need to spend hours in the dressing room beforehand, stuffing myself with padding and putting on a ton of makeup to conceal my identity."

"Do any of the customers suspect that you're not like the rest of your fellow performers?" Alek said.

"Not really," I chuckled. "They already have a hard enough time recognizing whether the other ones in my troupe are actually men."

"Are most of the people that come to your show *gay*?" Dmitri asked.

"Gay men and straight women," I nodded. "I think straight guys are a little embarrassed to be seen a gay club."

"You got that right," Dmitri laughed. "Which is unfortunate, because a lot of so-called straight men are actually bi-curious."

"That's certainly what I've found as an intersex woman," I said. "I'm constantly surprised by how quickly the straight guys that I date take a liking to my male anatomy when they discover I'm not just like a regular girl."

"How do you manage to hide your special features when you're performing?" Alek said, glancing at the crotch of my tight jeans while I sat kitty-corner to him on Olga's big sectional sofa.

"I don't have testicles like other men,' I said. "So it's easier for me to tuck my phallus between the folds of my pussy to keep it hidden. At least until it becomes *aroused*, when it seems to have a mind of its own."

"Can you show us a bit of your routine?" Dmitri said. "It seems only fair, since you've already seen us perform on the stage..."

I glanced at Olga for a moment, and she cocked her

head to the side, indicating it might be a good way to get all of us back in the mood.

"I suppose so," I said. "But it loses a bit of its effect when I'm dressed in tight jeans and a sweater. Can I borrow one of your dresses and something a little more revealing on the top?"

"Of course," Olga said, jumping up and grabbing my hand to drag her to her bedroom. "I think we can find something in my costume closet."

When we returned, I was wearing a knee-length bustle and lacy corset with high heels that made me look more like a saloon girl than a cabaret dancer, but I decided it would work for the purposes of a brief demonstration.

"Maybe we should play some *music* to set the mood," I said to Olga while I adjusted my breasts in the tight-fitting corset.

"Sure," she said, pulling out her phone and tapping on the Spotify app. "What did you have in mind?"

"Madonna's *Vogue* is always a good starting point," I smiled.

"One sec," Olga nodded, searching for the song on her app, then pairing her phone with her external speaker resting on the coffee table.

When the lyrics for the song started booming over the speakers, I began shimmying my hips and flapping my arms over my head like in the music video. While I strutted my body in front of the men sitting on the sofa, I noticed them shuffling their bodies uncomfortably as they changed the position of their legs, trying to hide their growing arousal. By the time the song ended, they both had flushed faces and large bulges in the front of their jeans.

"That was fun," Olga grinned, sitting between her colleagues on the sofa while she caressed the insides of their thighs. "You seem to have gotten a bit of a rise out of the spectators. Do you want to do one more number to open the gates all the way?"

"Mmm," I smiled, peering at their straining bulges. "I'd love to see that. Why don't we play *It's Raining Men* while I see if I can ramp up the excitement?"

Olga tapped her phone again, and when the new song started playing over the speakers, I strutted back and forth between the three of them, sitting side-by-side.

Hey! Hey! the song started.

We're the weather girls, uh-huh,

And have we got news for you,

Get ready all you lonely girls,

And leave those umbrellas at home...

As the men gaped at my bosom and my long, slender legs, I teased them by lifting my puffy skirt halfway while I pranced in front of them, watching their dicks tenting the front of their trousers even harder.

The humidity's rising, mm-hmm, the song continued,

The barometer's getting low,

According to all sources, the street's the place to go,

You better hurry up, 'cause tonight for the first time,

About half-past ten, it's gonna start raining men...

When the upbeat chorus began playing, I flicked my legs up in the air like a can-can girl, giving the others a teasing peak at my bare crotch, which I'd intentionally left uncovered to raise their excitement.

It's raining men!

Hallelujah, it's raining men!

I'm gonna go out to run,

And let myself get absolutely soaking wet,

Hallelujah, it's raining men!

The longer the song played, the more turned on I

became watching the men becoming increasingly aroused, until my cock was standing at full attention under my tenting skirt. When the last verse played and I suddenly turned around, bending over at the waist with my bustle hiked up over my hips to reveal my glistening pussy and eight-inch erection, Olga had already unzipped their pants while they played with their dripping dicks and their chests heaved in excitement.

"It looks like you've got everyone in the *mood*," she smiled as she grasped each of their hard-ons tightly with her hands. "What have you got planned for your next act?"

"Well," I said, unbuttoning my skirt and letting it fall to the floor while Dmitri and Alek stared at my throbbing instrument bobbing over my bare mound. "This is the *audience participation* part, where we go into the crowd to mix it up with the crowd. We can't let them have all the fun, can we?"

While the two men stared at my flapping hard-on and glistening labia, I walked closer to each of them, swiping the tip of my tool against their dripping crowns, making them groan loudly as thick drops of pre-cum slid out of their slits.

"Do you *like* what you see?" I smiled as they darted their eyes over my naked body.

"*God,* yes," Dmitri moaned, leaning forward as he tried to lick the end of my organ.

I pulled back and undid the laces of my corset until my breasts fell out the top of my bustier, revealing my pointed and erect nipples.

"Which part do you like the *most*?" I grinned, shimmying my hips next to them as I turned around and bent over to display my tight ass and pink pussy to both of the men.

"*All* of it," Dmitri panted, rocking his hips as his erection flapped inches away from my dripping opening.

"You're not *repulsed* by the sight of my pussy?" I teased him.

"Fuck, no," he grunted, grabbing the sides of my ass and pulling my hips closer to his burning pole. "With a dick like *that*, it's all the more appealing."

"Do you want to see what a *girl's* pussy feels like compared to a boy's?"

"Yes," he panted, raising his hips higher toward my perched ass.

I slowly lowered my hips over his dripping erection and when he felt my warm tunnel enveloping his organ, he curled his nails into the sides of my ass, rocking his torso forward to rest against my back. As I began to flex my leg muscles and pump my body up and down over his throbbing hard-on, he reached around my front and clasped my oversize dick with two hands, jerking it firmly while he fucked me from behind.

"What do you think?" I smiled as he plowed my ass. "Does it feel as good as a man?"

"Better," he groaned, squeezing my dick even harder as I felt his hot breath pouring over my back.

"I'm not sure which he's enjoying *more.*" Olga chuckled as she watched the two of us fucking on the sofa next to her and Alek. "Stroking your big dick, or fucking your wet ladyboy hole."

I glanced over at Alek, who was jerking his hard-on with two hands while he watched me fucking Dmitri next to him, then I paused for a moment, feeling Dmitri's hard-on pulsing on the edge of climax in my tight pussy.

"I think it's only fair that we share the spoils before we get too carried away," I said, pulling my hips off Dmitri's bouncing dick. "I don't want you guys popping off before everyone's had a kick at the can."

"I'd be happy to kick that can just about *anywhere*," Alek panted, alternating his attention between my flushed tits and my upturned erection bouncing over my shaved mound.

"Do you want to play with my *cock* while you fuck me?" I said, turning around to face him, with the tip of my organ bobbing inches away from his face.

"Yes," he grunted, parting his lips as he took my erection into his mouth. "But first, I'd rather *taste* it–"

"You see?" I said, turning toward Olga as she flicked her fingers over her clit while she watched Alek sucking my tool. "*Every* man likes my ladyboy cock, whether they're straight or they're gay."

"It's not just men," she panted as she trilled her pussy with her fingers. "I suspect just as many *women* are attracted to your sexy figure."

"Save that thought," I grinned as I reached out to squeeze her hard nipples. "Because I've got an idea how *all* of us can get in on the action after Alek loses his gay aversion."

Olga and Dmitri watched Alek sucking my dick while they played with themselves, and as I inched closer to climax, I contemplated shooting my jizz down his throat to test how much he'd switched allegiances. But I didn't want to come before everybody else had a turn, and I could tell from the deepening color of Alek's hard-on that he needed some attention on another part of his body.

"Whoa, there, big boy!" I said, pulling my throbbing pole out of his mouth. "You suck a dick like a champ, but I need to save a bit of energy if everyone's going to leave this party happy. Do you want to fuck me before we give Olga a turn?"

"Hell, yes," Alek panted as he wiped the back of his hand over the side of his dripping mouth. "How do you want to do it?"

"Well," I smiled back at him. "You seem to like my tits a little more than Dmitri, so why don't I sit on you facing forwards this time? That way, you can appreciate both my *feminine* and *masculine* sides at the same time."

"Oh my God," he shuddered, gaping at my hard-on dripping strings of pre-cum on top of my breasts. "Where have you been all my life?"

"Hiding in plain sight," I laughed as I tilted my hips upward and bent my knees, pointing my wet slit over his bobbing cock.

When I lowered myself over his organ and he felt my erection rubbing up against his torso, he wrapped his arms around my back and pulled me closer, moaning loudly in my ear.

"Are you starting to warm up to the idea of having sex with *boys*?" I grinned. "Or at least girls with *dicks*?"

"Either way works for me," he smiled, squeezing my tits while he rocked his hips against my slippery thighs. "It's all the more to play with..."

"Play with my cock," I said, peering down between our glistening bellies as I watched my purple crown sliding between our stomachs. "I want you to feel me spurting in your hands when you come inside me."

"What about *me*?" Olga interrupted us, tapping me on the back. "I thought you were going to *save* yourself until everybody had a turn?"

"Right," I said, tightening my leg muscles to stop the rocking action of Alek's and my body. "Although I didn't necessarily mean at the same time. But I have an idea how we might do that if you can find a larger surface for us to stretch out on."

"You're reading my mind, girl," Olga smiled, rising up off the sofa. "Let's move to the bedroom, where we can all have easier access."

Alek moaned in frustration when I lifted my pussy off his throbbing erection, but when I pulled his face toward my bosom, he sucked my nipples like a hungry baby.

"Mmm," I hummed when he slid two fingers into my

dripping hole and stroked my hard-on with his other. "*Now who's the one who's becoming more versatile?*"

I let him have his fun for a few moments until I felt the familiar pangs of a climax building up inside me, then I pulled my body back a few inches, displaying my throbbing erection for everyone to see.

"Jesus, girl," Olga panted while she stared at my large hard-on. "I think I undersold you when I was describing your virtues at the cafe."

"Not at all," Dmitri grinned, grabbing his balls while he stared at my glistening body. "She's everything you described, and more. I've never been this attracted to someone my whole life."

"Same here," Alek said, soaking up my body while he rolled his fingers over his dripping crown.

"That makes *three* of us," Olga chuckled, grabbing hold of Dmitri's and Alek's dicks and leading them into the bedroom.

When we entered her bedroom, the three others plopped onto the bed with their legs spread apart, wondering what I was going to do next.

"I don't know what you've got planned," Alek said. "But with all of that extra equipment you've got, we could position ourselves from pretty much any angle and get off rubbing ourselves against any part of your body."

"I had something a little different in mind," I chuckled. "Something where we're all rubbing the same parts together at the same time."

"How is that possible?" Olga said.

"You've heard of DP?" I smiled. "Well, I've always wanted to try *TP*, and this is finally my chance."

"TP?" Alek said. "You mean three cocks together? In one *pussy*?"

"Exactly," I nodded.

"Are you sure about that?" Olga said, wrinkling her forehead as she peered at our three throbbing erections. "It's hard enough getting *one* big cock in there, let alone two. But three cocks at the same time? I don't know if I can manage that..."

"If a woman's vagina can manage the passing of a baby's head through it, three cocks joined together can't be that big."

"In this case," she said, staring at my thick shaft. "I think it *is*. If not *larger*."

"Come on," I said, sitting on the mattress next to Dmitri and Alek while I spread my legs apart and bent my knees. "It will be fun to give it a try. You guys are *dancers*, right? With your flexibility and body acrobatics, anything should be possible."

"Okay," Alek nodded, shimmying his hips closer to me while we intertwined our legs.

Dmitri quickly followed suit, and within seconds, the three of us were sitting in a three-pointed star position, with our dicks joined together and our legs stretched out behind each of our asses.

"It looks like it's up to you to put the icing on the cake," I grinned toward Olga as she stared at our pyramid of three pricks with wide eyes. "Come kneel over top of us and let's see if we can make this work."

"Which way do you want me to face?" Olga said, squinting at the three of us.

"That's up to you," I smiled. "It depends if you'd prefer to get in touch with your masculine or feminine side while you fuck us."

"You already know the answer to that," Olga grinned as she crawled over toward us, lifting one knee and turning her body toward me while holding her dripping pussy over the tips of our throbbing dicks.

"Just go slowly at first," I nodded as she peered at me with frightened eyes. "Let your body adjust as you press down and breathe slowly."

"Just like when I'm having a *baby*?" she laughed.

"Exactly," I nodded.

"Except in this case, it's going *inside* my body, not out," she chuckled. "And I've got *three* people to satisfy, not just one."

"But you're much better *lubricated*," I grinned, feeling her juices dripping over the tip of my dick while she paused in excitement.

"Alright," she said, lowering her hips slowly. "Here goes nothing."

"When I felt the tip of my cock entering her hole, we groaned as she leaned forward to kiss me, rubbing our tits together softly.

"That's *one* down," she panted..

She hesitated when she felt the tip of Alek's slightly shorter phallus pressing against the front of her opening, then she grunted as she pressed her hips further down.

"It's a good thing you're sized differently," she smiled. "I can feel each of you stretching me in *increments*, instead of all at the same time."

"I'm glad it's not hurting," I said when I felt Alek's steaming pole sliding up next to mine as her slippery pussy enveloped our two organs. "Because it sure as hell feels good on my end."

"Mine too," Alek groaned as he slid his palms over the sides of Olga's trembling hips.

"I'm ready whenever you are," Dmitri said from the

opposite side as he waited patiently for Olga to squeeze his dick into her hole alongside mine and Alek's.

"Okay," Olga said, taking a deep breath and forcing her hips down over our three erections until we felt our dicks pressing up together in her tight pocket.

"Unghh," she groaned as she lowered her hips slowly while watching our faces contorting in pleasure.

"Is that a *good* sound or a bad sound?" I said, glancing at Olga with darted eyebrows.

"Mostly good," she panted as she slowly pushed her hips down until her dripping vulva rested against the base of our cocks. "A lot better than I imagine the feeling of a baby's *head* pushing me apart."

"Take your time," I groaned, feeling the pulses of the other men's heartbeats coursing through their hard-ons as Olga squeezed our poles together. "We're not going anywhere..."

"I suppose not," Olga said, kissing me softly on my lips. "You couldn't get out of there right now, even if you wanted to."

"Believe us when I say we *don't*," Alek chuckled.

"Yeah," Dmitri grunted. "This is the tightest hole I've ever been in, that's for sure."

"You don't mind that it's a *woman's* hole?" Olga said, turning her head to glance at Dmitri over her shoulder.

"Not in the least," he said. "I'm feeling more cocks right now than I ever have. This is the perfect joining of bodies, as far as I'm concerned."

"I'm glad you're enjoying it," Olga moaned as she started to raise and lower her hips slowly over our joined poles. "Because that's exactly what I was thinking."

"Yes, baby," I said, kissing Olga hard on the lips while she humped our cocks. "I can't wait to feel you gushing all over our bodies when you climax."

"I was already close to the edge from watching you earlier," Olga panted into my mouth. "It's not going to take long now. Are you guys almost ready to bust loose?"

"Fuck, yes," Alek said, tightening his legs around the back of our joined asses. "Just give me the word. I won't be able to hold it much longer..."

"Holy shit," Dmitri nodded, nearing the edge of climax. "This is the hottest thing I've ever done. I'm going to come so hard–"

"Oh my God," I gasped when I felt the two men's cocks beginning to pulse next to mine. "I can feel both of your poles pulsating. *Gahhhh!*"

When I felt my cock exploding next to Dmitri's and Alek's, I pulled our bodies together while I sprayed my pussy juices over their balls and Olga grunted in powerful waves of pleasure. None of us seemed to be able to stop coming, as wave after wave of powerful contractions consumed our bodies, and we shook together in one quivering mass of flesh. When we finally finished groaning in simultaneous ecstasy, we held each other tightly with our arms around each other's shoulders, heaving our bodies together in bliss.

"That was incredible," Dmitri panted, feeling his erection throbbing next to Alek's and mine. "You might have single-handedly turned me over to the other side. I'm going to have to call myself bisexual at the very least after this."

"I have to agree," Alek nodded while he pressed his balls against Dmitri's as they slid their dicks together in Olga's dripping tunnel. "That was a feeling I never even thought was possible."

"Well," Olga smiled as she placed her hands over our

shoulders and we pressed our foreheads together. "I wouldn't say I did it *single-handedly*. I had more than a little help from Shae–"

"You did most of the heavy lifting," I chuckled as I kissed my new partners on their cheeks. "I just added one extra ingredient to the picture."

"I dare say it was the most *important* ingredient," Olga nodded. "You're like the magnet that pulled all these polar opposites together. We couldn't have done this without you."

"I'm glad I helped pull the company together," I smiled. "Perhaps we should share our new technique with your artistic director? He won't have much room to criticize our form once he sees how perfectly we blend together."

"Fuck *that*," Dmitri said. "He can search for his *own* sexy pairing. There's not enough room to squeeze into our ensemble any more."

~

Ready for more ladyboy chills and thrills? Read the next volume in Shae's T-Girl Adventures: *The Nude Beach*. Buy direct and save at victoriarusherotica.com. Or download from your favorite online bookstore here: retailer links.

Turning more than just a few heads...

ALSO BY VICTORIA RUSH

Adult Fairytales:

The Enchanted Forest: An Erotic Fairytale

The Land of Giants: An Erotic Fairytale

The Dragon's Lair: An Erotic Fairytale

Witch's Brew: An Erotic Fairytale

The Mage's Spell: An Erotic Fairytale

The Mermaid Lagoon: An Erotic Fairytale

The Coven: An Erotic Fairytale

Rapunzel: An Erotic Fairytale

The Seven Dwarfs: An Erotic Fairytale

The Land of Mutants: An Erotic Fairytale

The Erotic Temple 1: A Sexy Fairytale

The Erotic Temple 2: A Sexy Fairytale

Erotic Fantasy:

Pirate's Bounty: A Time Travel Adventure

Wild West: A Time Travel Adventure

Private Riley: A Time Travel Adventure

Cleopatra's Secret: A Time Travel Adventure

Bounty Hunter 2125: A Time Travel Adventure

Ninja Assassin: A Time Travel Adventure

The 300: A Time Travel Adventure

Arabian Nights: An Erotic Fairytale (coming soon...)

Lesbian Erotica (Completed Series):

The Dinner Party: Lesbian Voyeur Erotica

The Darkroom: Bisexual Voyeur Erotica

Naked Yoga: Lesbian Transgender Erotica

Nude Cruise: Bisexual Voyeur Erotica

Rush Hour: Taboo Public Sex

The Girl Next Door: First Time Lesbian Erotic Romance

Girls' Camp: Lesbian Group Sex

Wet Dream: Ladyboy Fantasy Erotica

The Convent: Taboo Sex with a Nun

Sex Robot: A Dream Sex Machine

The Personal Trainer: Getting Pumped at the Gym

The Dominatrix: BDSM Lesbian Domination

Webcam Chat: Lesbian Online Sex

Paint Me: A Kinky Bodypainting Workshop

The Toy Party: Girls Sharing Sex Toys

The Costume Party: Strapping One On

Swedish Sauna: Lesbian Group Sex

The Therapist: Taboo Lesbian Erotica

Elevator Shaft: Bisexual Threesomes Erotica

Ladyboy: Lesbian Transgender Erotica

Peep Show: Lesbian Voyeur Erotica

The Dare: Public Sex Erotica

Maid Service: Lesbian Threesomes Erotica

The Hitchhiker: First Time Lesbian Erotica

The Housesitter: Spycam Lesbian Erotica

The Spa: Lesbian Group Orgy

Parlor Games: Blindfold Sex Party

The Exchange Student: First Time Lesbian Erotica

The Hostel: Bisexual Group Erotica

The Harem: Lesbian Erotic Romance

The Orient Express: Lesbian Voyeur Erotica

The First Lady: A Forbidden Lesbian Erotic Romance

The Slave: Lesbian BDSM Erotica

The Masseuse: Lesbian Sensuous Erotica

Too Close for Comfort: Lesbian Forbidden Erotica

Naked Twister: A Wild Party Game

Lexi: The Sex App (Lesbian Fantasy Erotica)

Call Girl: Lesbian Bisexual Threesomes Erotica

Circle Jill: Lesbian Masturbation Workshop

The Viewing Room: Masturbation Voyeur Erotica

Spin the Bottle: A Kinky Party Game

The Hair Salon: Lesbian Voyeur Erotica

Ladyboy Erotica:

The Auction: A Ladyboy Surprise

Hot Tub Hotel: Shemale Seduction

Strip Club for Couples: Transgender Erotica

Erotica Themed Bundles:

Voyeur: Lesbian Erotica Bundle

Public Affairs: A Lesbian Anthology

Futa Fantasies: The Ladyboy Collection

Threesomes: The Lesbian Collection

Threesomes - Volume 2: The Lesbian Collection

First Time: A Lesbian Anthology

Hedonism: An Erotic Anthology

Switch Hitters: Bisexual Erotica

Taboo Erotica: The Lesbian Series

BDSM: The Lesbian Collection

Party Games: The Erotic Collection

Party Games 2: The Erotic Collection

All Girl 1: Lesbian Erotica Bundle

All Girl 2: Lesbian Erotica Bundle

All Girl 3: Lesbian Erotica Bundle

All Girl 4: Lesbian Erotica Bundle

All Girl 5: Lesbian Erotica Bundle

All Girl 6: Lesbian Erotica Bundle

Voyeur: Volume 2

Erotic Fairytale Bundles:

Clover's Fantasy Adventures: Books 1 - 5

Clover's Fantasy Adventures: Books 6 - 10

Steamy Time Travel Bundles:

Riley's Time Travel Adventures: Books 1 - 5

Lesbian Erotica Bundles:

Jade's Erotic Adventures: Books 1 - 5

Jade's Erotic Adventures: Books 6 - 10

Jade's Erotic Adventures: Books 11 - 15

Jade's Erotic Adventures: Books 16 - 20